Did Cupid Make a Mistake or Is It Because Of Fate

Andrea Perico

Ukiyoto Publishing

All global publishing rights are held by

Ukiyoto Publishing

Published in 2023

Content Copyright © Andrea Perico

ISBN 9789360168247

*All rights reserved.
No part of this publication may be reproduced, transmitted, or stored in a retrieval system, in any form by any means, electronic, mechanical, photocopying, recording or otherwise, without the prior permission of the publisher.*

The moral rights of the authors have been asserted.

This is a work of fiction. Names, characters, businesses, places, events, locales, and incidents are either the products of the author's imagination or used in a fictitious manner. Any resemblance to actual persons, living or dead, or actual events is purely coincidental.

This book is sold subject to the condition that it shall not by way of trade or otherwise, be lent, resold, hired out or otherwise circulated, without the publisher's prior consent, in any form of binding or cover other than that in which it is published.

www.ukiyoto.com

Dedication

First of all, I want to thank God for providing me the courage, direction, and inspiration to write this poetry. Also, I want to express my gratitude to my family for their love and support.

Thank you, Ate Clarz, for believing in me and encouraging me all along the road as I pursued my writing career. You aren't just my best friend; you're also my companion, my sister, and my pal.

I'm grateful to Ukiyoto Publishing for making my greatest goal come true. I'm hoping you can assist other authors like me.

I'd also like to express my gratitude to Gem Ian, Moira, Sedi, Jem, Jazmine, Claire, Ashley Joy, Charisse, my cousins, Krista and many more. Thank you for always being there for me and supporting me; I'm grateful to each and every one of you.

Thank you to this particular individual who inspired me to compose this poetry; I'm glad I met you, but I guess some stories don't end the way we want it to end.

Finally, I'd like to congratulate myself; you finally did it, Drei, and I'm really proud of you.

Contents

Chapter I.	1
Chapter II.	2
Chapter III.	3
Chapter IV.	4
Chapter VI.	5
Chapter VII.	6
Chapter VIII.	7
Chapter IX.	8
Chapter X.	9
Chapter XI.	10
Chapter XII.	11
Chapter XIII.	12
Chapter XIV.	13
Apricity	14
Assurance	16
Chapter XVII.	18
Chapter X.	19
Chapter XIX.	20
Chapter XX.	21

Chapter XXI.	22
Chapter XXII.	23
Chapter XXIII.	24
Chapter XXIV.	25
Chapter XXV.	26
Chapter XXVI.	27
Chapter XXVII.	28
Chapter XXVIII.	29
Chapter XXIX.	30
Chapter XXX.	31
Chapter XXXI.	32
About the Author	33

Chapter I.

Your eyes shine
Through the night,
your smile brightens up
my darkest night.

Chapter II.

Being with you
It is something that I want too,
because of you
butterflies grew.

Chapter III.

One of the best
you're not less, I
admire you because you're
too good to be true.

Chapter IV.

We're close yet so far.
Just like a star
I'm contented to admire you
from afar.

Chapter VI.

Your smile brightens up my day
and I don't know what to say
It gives me hope and I pray
You look at me just how I look at you today.

Wishing that someday you'll choose me
Just how I chose you today.
I knew we can't be together,
I knew you love another
but I promise I can be better.

I will not hurt you just like what he did to you,
but I will not also force you to
love me too.

Chapter VII.

I'm here again in my room
thinking of what to do,
sitting all alone
because I don't know how
to deal with myself too.

Chapter VIII.

Writing a poetry
Isn't it lovely
to share your creativity
Oh!, what beautiful scenery.

Seeing that you do it gracefully
and that touch my heart emotionally
Sometimes you may feel melancholy,
but gladly you recover quickly.

Chapter IX.

I cry myself last night
and waking up in daylight.
What a beautiful sight
to see you loving someone new.

Chapter X.

Dissapearing like a bubble
I hate you for the trouble.

Chapter XI.

Missing you
is one thing I can't undo.

Chapter XII.

How can I move on ,
If you don't tell me
What's going on?

Chapter XIII.

You broke my heart yesterday, but now you're acting as if we're still ok.

Chapter XIV.

Seeing you brings back many memories that I intend to forget.

Apricity

Here I am again
sitting at the corner,
don't know what to do
because I'm exhausted too.
It's not rainy day but I feel
i'm tired every day.
Lost of motivation and inspiration
finding again my source of
happiness,
But when you came
It's like apricity, cause you
brighten my day
even on rainy days.
You're my remedy
because you are the reason for me
too wake up daily,
and facing another day without

disappointment and discouragement
Please stay by my side
because you're the reason
Why do I stand
Thank you for arriving
and meeting you cause now I'm
strong because of you.

Assurance

At first I didn't care even if you stared,

Pretending as if you're not there.

Turning a blind eye when you pass by,

but as the day goes by no matter how I try.

You're still stuck in my mind, and I know something doesn't feel right.

Still thinking of you every day and night, got lost in your eyes and I'm losing my mind.

So I'm asking myself why, why you suddenly caught my mind.

No matter how I try,

No matter what I do.

In the end I'm still thinking of you,

but there is something in you that makes me curious too.

In what way I caught your attention?, and why didn't you ask for my permission.

Do I look attractive to you?, or you're just judging me too.

Are you worth the risk?,

or I'm just assuming things.

How can I assure that my heart is secure if you yourself are not sure.

Chapter XVII.

I didn't even know if I ever fall in love again If it's not you.

Chapter X.

If a person wants you to stay,
then you would not beg for it.

Chapter XIX.

I hate that you make me wait,
every night you're late.
I wish you knew
how much I've been through
Just to wait for you.

Chapter XX.

I'm craving for someone.
Someone that will take care of me
Someone that willing to give his full attention to me
Someone that will encourage me and also
Someone that will love me.

Without asking him to give it
Without begging him to stay with me
because I deserve the same amount of love that I give.

Chapter XXI.

You just came into my life

unexpectedly without a warning

or a sign, that's why I don't know what to do because I'm still drown in my own thoughts too.

Chapter XXII.

I'm not selfish
but I'm not also selfless
I just want to cherish
the moments that we have
because I want my worries to be less,
and I want you to be happy too
cause you're my happiness.

Chapter XXIII.

I ghosted you
because I don't know
what to do.

I wanted to chat you
but I'm too confused,
I'm sorry for not being
brave to tell you the truth.

Chapter XXIV.

You're smiling
but I know deep inside you're
suffering, you're fighting
but I know it's tiring

Chapter XXV.

I'm starting to forget you
but deep inside I still like you.

Chapter XXVI.

Be proud for yourself
for overcoming your fear,
confessing to someone
who doesn't know you're
existing.

Chapter XXVII.

Even if the sun is shining brightly,
I still feel empty.

Chapter XXVIII.

The emptiness inside me are
slowly eating my energy.

Chapter XXIX.

Friendship first
but then they
ignore me.

I would like to understand
but it triggers me.

I tried to be calm
but my emotion
overcome me.

It's tiring and it drowns me,
the way I care for them
but they never care for me.

Chapter XXX.

Seeing you brings back many memories that I intend to forget.

Chapter XXXI.

Just like the daisy
you symbolize cheerfulness
but you're sad lately.

About the Author

Andrea Perico

Andrea is a wattpad aspiring author with the pen name Winx 29, she has 7 published stories, and she is also an NBD registered author. She is in her senior year of high school and is 18 years old. As a writer, she may not be able to write enough stories, but she's trying her best to share and inspire others through writing.

She has been dreaming of having her works published. But until then, She will continue inspiring her readers and other people around her as she take them to the magical world of her stories.

www.ingramcontent.com/pod-product-compliance
Lightning Source LLC
LaVergne TN
LVHW041559070526
838199LV00046B/2052